WILD
HEARTS

Adapted by Catherine Hapka

Based on the series created by Michael Curtis & Roger S. H. Schulman

Part One is based on the episode, "Fashion Victim," Written by Michael Curtis & Roger S. H. Schulman

Part Two is based on the episode, "Wrong Song," Written by Ivan Menchell

New York

visit us at www.abdopublishing.com

Reinforced library bound edition published in 2011 by Spotlight, a division of ABDO Group, 8000 West 78th Street, Edina, Minnesota 55439. This edition reprinted by arrangement with Disney Press, an imprint of Disney Book Group, LLC. www.disneybooks.com

Printed in the United States of America, Melrose Park, Illinois.
042010
092010
 This book contains at least 10% recycled materials.

Library of Congress Cataloging-in-Publication Data
This title was previously cataloged with the following information:

Hapka, Catherine.
 Wild Hearts / Adapted by Catherine Hapka.
  p. cm. (Jonas ; #1)
 I. Title. II. Series: Jonas.

[Fic]--dc22   2009920715

ISBN 978-1-59961-738-1 (reinforced library edition)

All Spotlight books have reinforced library binding and are manufactured in the United States of America.

PART ONE

CHAPTER ONE

"You know what my favorite part about the end of a tour is?" Kevin Lucas mused. He hung up one of his guitars alongside hundreds of others on a revolving rack. Not bothering to wait for his younger brothers Joe and Nick to respond, he immediately answered his own question. "It's getting off the tour bus with those stacked beds, the traffic sounds all night, the flashing headlights . . ." He made a face, then flopped down on a bunk bed and closed the curtains that surrounded the mattress. "Aaaah! It's good to be home."

Kevin was in one of the bunk beds running along the wall and made to look exactly like those on their tour bus. When he reached over and flipped a switch, traffic noises poured out of a speaker. Lights started flashing like passing head-lights. Apparently, home was a tour bus without wheels.

Nick wasn't paying attention. He was used to his flighty brother. Instead, he was bent over his synthesizer. The room he shared with Joe and Kevin in the loft of their family's converted-firehouse home was a mess, but as usual, Nick was totally focused on his music.

Unpacking from JONAS's latest tour would have to wait. Never mind that suitcases and duffel bags were everywhere, that there was a drum set plunked in the middle of the room, and that clothes covered every available surface—from the beds to the vending machines. He and his brothers were in one of the hottest bands out there. And, true, there were fame, fans, and plenty of fun, but there was also the big *R*—responsibility. Sometimes, Nick thought, he was the only one in the group to take the big *R* seriously—musically at least.

"Could you guys keep it down?" Nick asked. "I've got to finish these new songs for the next album."

Joe was the only one doing any actual unpacking. Pushing his long, dark hair out of his face, he glanced over at Nick and rolled his eyes. "You're already working on new songs? We've been home for, what, ten minutes?"

"Yeah, and I'm not even done with the second song yet!" Nick bit his lip. "I hope I don't have writer's block."

The curtains parted in front of Kevin's bunk bed. He yawned and hopped out. "Ah, nothing like a power nap," he said. "What city are we in?"

Joe ignored him. He'd just opened another

suitcase and found a teddy bear inside. It was wearing a hat and a loose-fitting tie.

"Here's Frankie Bear," he told the others. Then he glanced around the loft with a worried frown. Something wasn't right. "Wait a minute. Where's Frankie?"

Frankie was the youngest Lucas brother, which pretty much made him JONAS's unofficial mascot. He went everywhere with his older brothers, including on tour. The trouble was, the last time Joe had seen Frankie had been . . . uh, when? He couldn't quite remember. On the tour bus that morning? Maybe. Or maybe not. After their last show the night before? He couldn't quite remember. . . .

Suddenly Frankie popped out of a bass drum. He was dressed just like the teddy bear.

"How long have you been in there?" Nick asked him.

Frankie grinned. "Since your last drum solo."

Just then, their father, Tom Lucas, came up the stairs to the loft. "Hey, Frankster," he greeted his youngest son as Frankie scurried past. "Haven't seen you since—"

"We were playing hide-and-seek!" Frankie reminded him.

"Oh, right." Mr. Lucas shot him a slightly guilty smile. "Sorry about that. I guess you win." As Frankie rushed out, Mr. Lucas turned to the older boys. "Mom told me to tell you to clean out the tour bus and do your dirty laundry," he said. "And I should warn you, she had that 'clean out the tour bus and do your dirty laundry' look on her face."

"But there's ten weeks of dirty laundry on that bus!" Kevin protested. "And we go back to school on Monday. It's our last weekend of freedom—we want to go wild!"

Nick nodded. "You know, do something crazy!"

"Like sleep," Joe added with a yawn. He was already having visions of long, uninterrupted hours and hours of rest . . .

Their father smiled. "I'll fix it with Mom. But

first thing in the morning, you're doing the laundry. Before those clothes go out on tour by themselves." Turning, he left to go and report back to his wife.

When Mr. Lucas had gone, Kevin grinned at his brothers. "Hey, if our clothes are going on tour, I should warn Dad my leather pants can't play guitar very well."

They hadn't been alone long when Stella Malone hurried in from the direction of the closet. Stella was pretty, perky, plucky, and blond. She had known the Lucas brothers forever. But she wasn't just their lifelong friend and high school classmate. She wasn't even only both those things *plus* their most loyal fan. She was also JONAS's superstylin' fashion consultant. Stella didn't follow the trends—she *made* them. With her help, JONAS always looked as awesome as they sounded.

"Okay," Stella said briskly, walking over to a touch-screen computer mounted on one wall, "I've loaded all your clothes into what I like to call the Stellavator." She looked at the piles of laundry and added silently, *clean* clothes. "Patent pending. Check it out."

Nick finally looked up from his keyboard. Joe tossed aside the suitcase he was unpacking. Kevin stopped looking sleepy. All three wandered over. Stella was always coming up with cool fashion-related inventions. They couldn't wait to see the latest.

When she was sure she had their attention, Stella touched a button and turned on the screen. "I've cross-referenced everything by brother, season, occasion, and fashion curve—which, as usual, thanks to me, we're ahead of," she explained. "For example, Joe—"

She touched the screen. An image of Joe popped up. He was dressed in boxers and a tank top—fashionable ones, of course.

"It's Saturday night," Stella said, pressing the screen again. "It's a movie premiere. It's summertime."

A rockin' outfit appeared on the on-screen

Joe. Then Stella hit another button. From the back wall of the loft, a clothing rack slid out. Hanging on that rack was the same outfit. All three brothers looked amazed.

"That is *sick*!" Kevin cried. "Do one for me!"

Stella nodded and touched the screen again. This time an image of Kevin appeared.

"Weekend, photo shoot, spring," Stella said, tapping the screen to reveal a funky outfit.

"Too cool!" Kevin exclaimed. "But wait, I want different pants."

He lunged past Stella and jabbed at the screen with his fingers. Immediately, a piercing alarm sounded. NOT APPROVED! the screen blinked in big, red, disapproving letters. SEE STELLA.

"No clashing allowed," Stella scolded. "Any change must be approved through my department. Which is me."

Nick chuckled. "Cool. Are these pants okay to get something to eat?" He waved a hand at what he was wearing. "'Cause I'm starving."

"Want to come with?" Joe asked Stella.

"Love to, but I have to replace the knees in all of Kevin's pants." Stella shot Kevin a look. "Why do you *insist* on power-sliding across stage every night?"

"Because I'm awesome," Kevin replied proudly.

Stella sighed. She should have known better than to ask.

CHAPTER TWO

It was Monday morning. After weeks on the road, going back to school seemed exotic and cool to the Lucas brothers. Well, sort of cool anyway. Okay, maybe not that cool at all. It was noisy and crowded and smelled like books and gym shorts. But, for the most part, they were happy to be back at Horace Mantis Academy.

The hallway was hopping as students rushed around, catching up or just getting ready for the day.

The Lucas brothers were at their lockers when Stella ran up to them. "Sorry I'm late," she said, panting.

Joe smiled, relieved to see her. When she hadn't showed at her usual time, he'd been afraid that fixing the knees on all of Kevin's pants the night before had made her run amuck. He wasn't sure exactly where "amuck" was, but he had heard it on TV once and was convinced it was nowhere good.

"Hey," he said. "I was worried about you."

Stella touched his arm. "Really?"

Joe felt his face go red. He hadn't meant it *that* way. Why did seeing Stella always make him say goofy things? He didn't get it. He wasn't like that at all around other girls. No way. With most girls, he wasn't just Joe—he was Joe Cool.

"I mean, you know, *we* were all worried," he stammered. "Right, guys?"

"Uh, sure," Kevin said, shrugging. He hadn't even noticed that Stella was late.

"Okay," Nick said, absentmindedly. He was

more focused on trying to load his keyboard into his locker than on the conversation.

Unaware of Joe's attempt to cover up, Stella pulled out a sketch book. "Okay," she said, all business. "In a couple of days, we're flying to England to meet the prime minister so he can personally thank you for those charity concerts you did."

Kevin scratched his head. "I know this prime minister guy is, like, the president of England," he said. "But I forgot what they told us to call him. Primey?"

"I'm going to call him Primo," Joe said.

Nick rolled his eyes. His brothers could be so . . . well, brotherly. "We just call him Prime Minister," he said matter-of-factly.

Stella didn't care about any of that. The brothers could call the guy Prime Rib for all she cared. *She* was all about the clothes.

"I designed a new look for you," she told them. "The whole world will be watching. You have to look amazing for this ceremony."

Before she could go on, a shadow fell across the floor. A moment later a voice said, "Hey, Stella."

Joe turned to see who had just spoken. It was Van Dyke Tosh. True, Van Dyke was one of their classmates, but Joe didn't know him that well. Probably because they didn't have much in common. While Joe and his brothers were out being music superstars, Van Dyke was busy being the superstar of the school football team. Not to mention a legend in his own mind. And *only* his mind, Joe said to himself.

Stella had turned and seen Van Dyke, too. Taking in the athlete's handsome features, her face lit up like one of the spotlights from a JONAS stage show.

"Hi there, Van Dyke!" she exclaimed.

Joe narrowed his eyes suspiciously. Was it just him, or did her voice suddenly sound extragirly?

"Thanks for the study help this morning," Van Dyke told Stella, leaning one jocklike shoulder oh-so-casually against the nearest locker. "I can

13

take down two linebackers at once, but I can't tackle Shakespeare."

Stella laughed. A little too hard, in Joe's opinion. Nick and Kevin just rolled their eyes. It was a pretty lame joke.

"Van Dyke, you're so funny!" Stella gushed. "It was just your standard 'discuss five opposites in *Romeo and Juliet.*'"

"Yeah," Van Dyke said. "But before you came along, all I could come up with was 'Juliet's a girl, Romeo's a dude.'"

Stella laughed again. Usually Joe liked hearing Stella's laugh. It was happy and bubbly and made everyone around her feel good. But not today. Today her laugh sounded weird. It was sort of getting on his nerves, actually. Especially since nothing Van Dyke was saying was funny. Nothing at *all*.

"Stop it, Van Dyke!" Joe howled, practically doubling over with fake laughter. "You're making my sides hurt!" Then he went serious again, his eyes narrowed. "We were just having a business meeting about how we're flying to England to meet the prime minister."

"England." Van Dyke grinned at Stella, totally ignoring Joe's glare. "Home of Shakespeare, right?

"Right!" Stella beamed at him.

"We make a good team," Van Dyke said.

Team? Joe silently fumed. She answered your silly, rhetorical question! How does this make you a team? And why am I so bugged by it?

Stella clearly shared none of Joe's concerns. She giggled and did a quick little rah-rah move. "Yay, team!"

Now even Nick and Kevin were concerned. They traded a look. Yay, team? Who was this weird girl, and what had she done with level-headed Stella?

Joe frowned. "Can we get back to reality, please?" he snapped. "As in us looking amazing for our ceremony?"

Van Dyke finally seemed to take the hint. "Stay beautiful," he said to Stella as he strutted off, a random group of giggling girls following behind him.

Stella watched him go. For a long time.

"Stella?" Kevin said at last.

"Huh?" She blinked. "Oh, sorry."

Joe was still frowning. This was new. And totally bizarre. Stella didn't go all gaga over guys like Van Dyke. At least she never had before. And in Joe's opinion, this was no time to start. Couldn't she see Van Dyke wasn't anywhere near good enough for her? For Pete's sake—he was wearing *synthetic fibers*!

"It's cool that you're tutoring Van Dyke," Joe said, trying to sound like he meant it. "But I hope you haven't forgotten you're helping me with my math tonight."

"Of course I'm not going to forget," Stella said. "You're my special project."

That made Joe feel a little better. "'Special project,'" he echoed, smiling at her. "I like that."

Nick sighed. "If you two are done being adorable, can we get back to the meeting?"

"Sorry." Stella reached into her backpack and pulled out a photo. "Take a look at these pants."

"Those are cool," Joe said.

"Aren't they?" Stella smiled, going all dreamy-eyed again. "Van Dyke wears them."

"Cool, except for the color, fabric, design, and belt loops," Joe corrected himself smoothly. "On second thought, I hate them."

CHAPTER THREE

Later that day, Joe was on his way to class when he heard Stella's voice from around the corner. He was about to walk over to say hi. But then he heard her say a name.

"And then Van Dyke said we make a great team!" she said happily.

"No way!" Joe recognized the voice of Stella's friend Macy Misa.

"*So* way," Stella replied.

"Go 'way!" Macy exclaimed.

Their voices were getting closer. Joe couldn't help it—he was curious to hear more.

He shot a look around the hallway. Aha! There was the perfect hiding place for a little undercover work. . . .

From his hiding spot, Joe watched Stella and Macy round the corner. Stella looked completely blissful. "I can't believe Van Dyke thinks he and I make a great team." Joe rolled his eyes as Stella took a sip from the juice box she was holding. He noticed it was the same kind of juice Van Dyke had been drinking earlier that day.

Clearly, Macy had other boys on the brain. "*I* can't believe you got to smell Nick up close," Macy said wistfully, clutching her binder to her chest. She was the world's biggest JONAS fan. "I've always imagined he smells like chocolate-chip cookies. Sugar-free, of course. On the other hand, I bet Kevin smells like heaven. It's true because it rhymes."

Stella smiled at her friend. Macy was a star

athlete. On the soccer field, the tennis court, or the javelin pitch, she was as tough as nails and as cool as a cucumber. But she got a little squeaky and squooshy when the subject of the JONAS guys came up. Never mind how she acted whenever she saw them in person—that could be downright embarrassing and often ended in fainting. Still, it didn't stop Macy from being the president of their fan club and from knowing almost everything there was to know about JONAS.

But Stella wasn't concerned with any of those boys. At the moment, she was all about Van Dyke. "And the best part," she told Macy, "is Van Dyke asked me out. Tonight, he's taking me to see *Pretty Princess II 3-D: Crowns A-Poppin'*."

Macy let out a squeal. "That's, like, a total chick flick!" she cried. "No guy would take a girl to that on purpose."

Both of them were so caught up in their conversation they didn't notice that one of the school's large trash cans was moving. They didn't even notice when the walking trash can almost bumped into a passing student or two.

Undercover work was harder than it looked. Inside, Joe tried not to scream. A chick flick? What was Van Dyke trying to prove?

"Van Dyke would." Stella sighed happily. "He's so romantic! I can't believe I'm going out with the cutest guy in school."

"Correction: *fourth* cutest." Macy opened her binder and whipped out a full-color 3-D pop-up of JONAS onstage. She'd made it herself. Every detail was perfect, from the way Joe held the microphone to the angle of Kevin's sideburns to every last curl on Nick's head.

Stella checked it out. It was definitely among Macy's most impressive JONAS-related work so far. "Cool," she said. "Can you make a pop-up of me and Van Dyke?"

Macy shrugged. "Yeah, after I'm done grouting my life-size JONAS mosaic."

Stella took the last sip of her juice. "Just a sec," she said, turning to go back to the trash can they had passed.

But she had to stop short to avoid tripping over that same trash can. For some reason, it was right behind her instead of halfway back down the hall where it belonged. That was weird. But it wasn't really worth worrying about. Not when she had a hot date with Van Dyke later. She tossed the juice box in and turned away.

As the girls disappeared around the next corner, Nick and Kevin appeared. Kevin took the last bite of the banana he was eating. He walked over and tossed the peel into the trash can. Then he did a double-take.

"Were you just asking me where Joe was?" he asked Nick.

"Yeah."

Kevin gestured to the trash can. "Found him."

Nick yanked the lid off the can. Joe was crouched inside. And he was wearing Kevin's discarded banana peel like a hat. A slimy, yellow hat.

"You don't think Stella would blow me off for

a date with Van Dyke, do you?" Joe asked his brothers anxiously.

"Huh, that's a tough one," Nick said, thoughtfully stroking his chin. "Captain of the football team . . . Guy in a trash can wearing a banana-peel hat . . ." Nick shrugged. "I'm stumped."

"Tonight's the night she's supposed to help me with my math," Joe whined.

Kevin shook his head. "Dude, I think your biggest math problem is, Joe plus trash can equals bonkers."

Joe sighed. When his older brother was right, he was right. He had hit an all-time low.

CHAPTER FOUR

That night, Joe set out his math books in the loft, ready for his study session. Then he sat back and waited for Stella. And waited. Then he waited some more. He glanced around the room. He needed a distraction. His brothers weren't around, but their clothes were. A portable clothing rack was standing in the middle of the room. It held a bunch of stylish outfits and a sign reading: FOR PRIME MINISTER MEET & GREET.

24

The clothes made him think of Stella—again. Where was she? He checked his watch and sighed.

Suddenly, the phone rang and Joe quickly answered. "Hello? Oh, hey, Stella. Where are you? I've got the chapter on decimals open, and it says you're fifteen-point-two-five-eight minutes late," he said, trying to sound playful. It didn't really work. He listened for a moment. "Yeah, I know Van Dyke. . . . Yeah, I hear that's a great movie. I wanted to see it, too." He listened again, his face falling. "Sure, we can do it some other night. Have a blast. Bye."

Joe hung up, totally bummed. So much for being Stella's "special project" . . .

He slammed his math book shut, then reached for the remote. The TV in the loft got a gazillion channels—he had to be able to find something to distract him from Stella's crazy, un-Stella-like behavior. Isn't that why cable had been invented? But as he flipped through channel after channel, all he seemed to see on any of them was Stella's face. And Van Dyke's.

Then he stopped on a commercial. "In a world of fairy dust and unicorn sneezes," the announcer declared, "one young 3-D girl will teach an entire kingdom that only a ruler who loves can love a lover who rules. Kate Laceylips and Owen Smeldrake are *Pretty Princess II 3-D: Crowns A-Poppin'*!"

Joe squeezed his eyes shut. He could see it now: Stella and Van Dyke hugging and dancing and tiptoeing through stupid unicorn meadows together. . . . Ugh! What in the world could Stella possibly see in a guy like that? Joe just. Did. Not. Get. It.

Not that it mattered *that* much, of course. He was simply concerned for Stella's well-being. As a friend. Totally. Without a doubt. No questions asked.

Just then, Kevin and Nick came in, unaware of Joe's internal freak-out. Spotting the clothes rack, Kevin hurried over to check it out.

"Is that the stuff we're wearing to meet

26

the prime minister?" he asked.

Nick hurried after him. "Don't touch," he warned. "Stella said hands off until we have to wear it." Finally, he noticed Joe sitting there staring at the TV with a goofy look on his face. "Dude, get your jacket," he said. "We're hitting the movies."

"We're seeing *Velocity Overkill!*" Kevin added, his eyes bright.

Nick nodded eagerly. "There's a scene where there's a car jumping over a car—that's *jumping over another car!*" he told Joe.

Joe did not look excited. "What's with everybody going to the movies?" he grumbled. "You, Stella . . ."

"Oh, right," Kevin said. "She went to that chick flick with Van Dyke."

"She's supposed to be *here*, helping *me* with important math!" Joe complained.

"Dude," Kevin said, "I think your biggest math problem is—"

"Don't." Nick held up a hand to stop him. The

27

joke hadn't even been that funny the first time. Then he turned to Joe. "Why can't you study with Stella on a different night?"

Joe gritted his teeth. His brother was totally missing the point. Who cared about studying? Studying wasn't the point. Studying was so totally beside the point, it might as well be in a different zip code from the point.

"She should be here anyway!" he snapped, losing his temper.

"Why?" Kevin asked, confused.

Now that he thought about it, Joe wasn't really sure why. But he knew his brothers wouldn't accept that answer. He had to respond carefully. Otherwise, they'd start thinking he was *jealous* or something lame like that. And Stella was a friend. Just a friend.

He glanced around for a good response. "Guarding the clothes!" he blurted out as his gaze fell on the clothing rack. "We have to wear this stuff to meet the *prime minister of England*! What if something happens to it? It could cause an international incident!"

Nick smirked. "I get it now," he said. "You're jealous."

"Jealous?" Joe exclaimed. "Of who?"

"Van Dyke and Stella," Kevin observed, seeing exactly where Nick was going.

Joe shook his head. "Van Dyke's a dwonk!" he cried. "And Stella? Please! She's got all that blond hair. And her skin is perfect. And she laughs at all my jokes. Gross!"

Kevin glanced at Nick and said, "Poor lad. He's so jealous he's oozing green."

Joe glared at Kevin. Why weren't they taking this more seriously?

"What if someone broke in?" Joe demanded. Spying a pen lying on the table by his books, he grabbed it and waved it around. "And they had a pen? And they started swirling it around. They could ruin our new clothing!"

"You mean like you just did?" Nick said, nodding at the clothes.

Joe's eyes grew wide. In all his crazy

pen-brandishing, he had just left a huge mark on one of the brand-new shirts! He was in big trouble.

"Stella's going to kill us!" Joe moaned.

"*Us?*" Kevin said. "You're taking the heat for this one alone, Mr. Jealous."

"I am *not* jealous!" Joe exclaimed.

Kevin shrugged. "Whatever. Bye, Jealous Boy."

"Leave him alone," Nick told Kevin.

Kevin shrugged again. Then he headed for one of the three fire poles leading downstairs. Grabbing it, he slid out of sight.

Nick got ready to follow, but he couldn't resist. "See ya, Jealous," he added, before sliding down the fire pole after his brother.

All too quickly, Joe was alone with his pen. And the ruined shirt. He stared from one to the other, feeling panicky. What would Stella say when she saw what he'd done? Or would she say *anything*? Nope, she'd probably never talk to him again!

The panic was making it hard to think

straight. He had to do something—anything—to fix this. Quickly, he grabbed the hanger holding the shirt and reached into Stella's handy bag of touch-up stuff. . . .

CHAPTER FIVE

An hour later, Nick and Kevin raced into the loft, wide-eyed and breathless. Kevin was clutching a jumbo tub of popcorn.

Nick spotted Joe pacing back and forth. "We got your nine-one-one," Nick said, panting. "What's the emergency?"

"Are Mom and Dad okay? Where's Frankie?" Kevin cried. It looked like nothing was on fire, so he glanced around wildly, expecting to see their parents or younger brother lying there bleeding or something.

Just then Stella rushed in. She looked amazing. Her outfit was even more stylish than usual. It totally said "I'm on a hot date, but I'm too cool to care."

"I got here as soon as I could!" she cried breathlessly.

"What took you all so long?" Joe said. He glanced at Stella. "Especially you."

"Joe, what is it?" Nick insisted.

"We have a fashion emergency," Joe said grimly.

Kevin relaxed. Some emergency! "Are you talking about the pen mark?" he asked.

"Pen mark?" Stella echoed with concern in her voice.

Nick glanced at her. "Joe got a pen mark on his new shirt for the prime minister meet-and-greet."

"What?" Stella squawked. "That shirt's one of a kind!"

"It was an accident!" Joe protested.

Stella took a deep breath. "It's all right," she said, sounding calmer already. "I can get it out. Where's the shirt?"

She looked around for the clothing rack. It was still there. But the clothes weren't. The rack was empty.

"Where's *everything*?" she asked, a note of panic creeping back into her voice.

"Okay, here's what happened," Joe said quickly. "By the way, anyone want anything? Soft drink? Chips?"

Stella had known the Lucas brothers a long time. She recognized that look on Joe's face. And it meant trouble with a capital *T*. And a capital *R-O-U-B-L-E*, too. With an exclamation point at the end. Maybe two.

"*What happened to the clothes?*" she demanded.

"Okay, I got a pen mark on the shirt," Joe said. He had to make this all sound very convincing. "But I figured I could get it out. But I couldn't. So I put it in the wash."

"You put that shirt in the wash?" Stella cried.

Didn't the words "dry-clean only" mean anything to him?

Apparently not, as Joe was still talking. "And that just turned it blue," he explained. "And then it didn't match the pants anymore, so I figured I'd put the pants in the wash."

Stella gasped in horror. "You put the *pants* in the wash?"

"Then nothing matched anything, so I put everything in the wash."

"*AAAAAAAAAAH!*" Stella screamed.

Kevin rushed over to her. "Stella, take slow, deep breaths," he advised helpfully. "Imagine a peaceful forest. With bunnies . . . kittens . . . and no washing machines."

"Joe," Nick said, "where are all the clothes now?"

Joe pointed. "In that soggy pile in the corner."

Stella looked. And immediately wished she hadn't. She'd never seen anything so shocking and tragic in her life. Oh, the humanity . . . It was

CHAPTER SIX

"**O**kay, I'm not sure," Stella said a couple hours later. "But I *think* I may be a genius." She slid one last shirt into place on the clothing rack and stepped back to survey her work. "A whole new wardrobe and there's still two hours before we have to meet the plane."

"It's going to look great, Stell," Nick said. He and his brothers had been watching Stella put together the new outfits for the prime minister meet-and-greet. Well, he and Kevin had been watching. Joe had been sulking. Stella had still gone on her date, she was upset with him, *and* his first outfit—which he had totally loved—was now ruined.

"Joe, I don't get it," Stella said after she had taken one last look at her new masterpieces. "If you didn't like the outfit I put together for you, all you had to do was tell me instead of ruining everything."

"It *was* an accident!" Joe protested for the umpteenth time. "I *loved* those outfits. I even told the guys you should've been here guarding them instead of going out on a *date* with some *guy*."

Stella blinked, looking puzzled. "Is that what this is about? You're jealous of Van Dyke taking me out?"

"Yes," Kevin and Nick replied in unison.

"No!" Joe exclaimed at the same time.

Stella narrowed her eyes at him. This picture was getting a whole lot clearer. "Did you ruin everybody's clothes *on purpose*?"

"No!" Joe exclaimed again.

"But you ruined *your* suit on purpose," Stella guessed.

"No!"

Stella was starting to get exasperated. "But you marked up your shirt with a pen on purpose."

"No comment." Joe hesitated, then shrugged. "Accidentally on purpose."

"Because?" Stella prompted.

Joe frowned. "I didn't want you going out with Van Dyke," he blurted out. "I heard really nasty things about him. He . . . uh, combs his hair against the natural part."

Stella took a deep breath. When she spoke, her voice was calm. Eerily calm.

"So you ruined my date with the guy I've been waiting a month to ask me out," she said, "for my own good?" She took a shirt off the rack and handed it to Joe. "That's so sweet of you to worry about me."

Joe was relieved. Stella seemed to be okay. "You're welcome. So we're cool?"

"Of course," Stella said sweetly, all the while gritting her teeth. "Go try that on."

Joe hurried off to the dressing area, completely oblivious. That had been a close one. . . . Maybe now Stella would come to her senses and dump Van Dork.

Meanwhile Nick and Kevin were watching Stella carefully. They weren't nearly as clueless as their brother. "Pretty mad at Joe, huh?" Nick said.

Kevin just watched, taking a sip of the tea he'd poured for himself. Ugh. It was cold. But he didn't dare step over to pour himself a new cup. He didn't want to turn his back on Stella when she looked like that. Just in case.

"Why would you say that?" Stella said to Nick, her voice still calm. Very, *very* calm.

Kevin glanced at the clothes hanger she was holding. She was clutching it so hard that it was glowing red. And smoking. He reached over and dipped one end in his tea cup. Steam poured out of it.

Seeing how distraught Stella was, Nick had an idea. A potentially entertaining idea. Sometimes life off the road could be dull . . . maybe it was time to add some spice. "Wow. Ruining all our clothes, messing up Stella's date," Nick mused. "I think somebody needs to be taught a lesson."

Kevin perked up at that. "If that fancy talk means having some fun with Joe, I'm in!" he said immediately.

Stella looked at them. "Have I ever told you guys I love you?" she said, her mouth twitching into a smile. An evil, evil smile.

Kevin and Nick smiled back. Evil, evil smiles. This was going to be fun. . . .

CHAPTER SEVEN

The headquarters of the Prime Minister of England was a prim and proper place. Its hallways were hushed. Its tea trays were polished. Its stuff was stuffy. It was the kind of place where you expected Mary Poppins to appear any moment.

But one of the anterooms was looking rather less British than usual. That was because the three members of JONAS were using it as a dressing room. They'd brought in director's chairs, a portable makeup table with a long, lighted mirror, and a curtained-off changing area.

Kevin and Nick were lounging in two of the director's chairs. A hair-and-makeup artist was touching up their faces and fluffing their flawless 'do's. It was almost time for their meeting with the prime minister, and everything needed to be perfect.

Mr. Lucas entered, accompanied by a bodyguard. As his sons' manager, he had to be around at all times. The bodyguard with him was big. Really big. That's why everyone called him the Big Man. The Big Man scanned the room for signs of danger while Mr. Lucas stepped over to talk to his sons.

"Have a good one, guys," he said. "Nick, keep it light. Kevin, don't embarrass America. You both look great." He glanced over at the bodyguard. The Big Man had failed to locate anything dangerous, so now he was standing at the alert. If danger *did* appear, he would be ready. He was always ready. "When the Big Man says go," their father added, "you go."

The Big Man gave them a look. Then he and Mr. Lucas left.

A moment later, Stella appeared, hurrying over to the curtained-off dressing area. "Joe," she said to the curtain, "are you having trouble finding your outfit? I laid it out on the chair."

Joe stuck his head out. "But this isn't the outfit I had on at home!" he said, sounding worried.

"I know," Stella replied. "But luckily, when you accidentally-on-purpose ruined your shirt, it gave me a brainstorm."

Joe's head disappeared back behind the curtain. Stella glanced at Nick and Kevin and smiled. Then all three of them waited.

Soon Joe appeared again. All of him, this time. "Okay." He sounded confused as he looked down at his clothes. "But am I wearing this right?"

Kevin and Nick had to work hard not to crack up when they saw him.

Joe looked like something straight out of the circus. No, more like some old glam rocker from sometime around, oh, 1974. Gold. Tassels.

Oversized sunglasses. And sequins—oh, yes, there were sequins.

Joe was still staring down at himself. Normally he totally trusted Stella's fashion sense. But if this was the latest trend, he had to admit he didn't get it.

"This seems kind of . . . out there," he said. Then he noticed his brothers staring at him. They were wearing the same totally cool and normal outfits Stella had picked out the day before. "Why aren't *they* wearing this?"

"Oh, we could never pull this off," Kevin responded quickly.

Nick nodded. "This look is totally Joe," he added.

"It's all the rage in England," Stella put in. "Super–cutting edge."

"*This* is cutting edge?" Joe asked, in disbelief.

"If there's any edge to cut, you're cutting it right now," Nick replied.

"Like, *ouch*," Kevin agreed.

Joe looked at himself in the mirror over the

makeup table. Okay, so at first sight he looked ridiculous. But maybe he was thinking like someone who was totally trend-impaired. Was the outfit really ridiculous—or ridiculously awesome?

Stella knows what she's doing, Joe reminded himself. She's, like, the crown princess of fashion. Besides, she said this outfit is superhot in England. What's that saying? When among the British, do as the British do, right?

"Okay, I see it now!" he said, trying to psych himself up. "Sure."

Then he paused. He looked in the mirror again. A gold sequin caught the light, making him squint.

"Really?" he said, the doubts creeping back. "Stella, I don't know about this. . . ."

"Of course you do," Stella said briskly. She pointed to the door. "In thirty seconds, you've got a date with the Prime Minister of England. And nothing's going to break that date except an emergency." She cocked an eyebrow at him.

"Have you got an emergency that's going to break a date, Joe?"

Joe blinked. Were the sequins blinding him, or was she . . . glaring at him? Why was she glaring?

"Do you think he gets it?" Kevin asked Nick.

"Be patient," Nick replied. "Five, four, three . . ."

"Wait a minute!" Joe blurted out, suddenly realizing something.

"Two, one . . ." Nick went on.

"You *are* mad at me!" Joe said to Stella.

Nick smiled. "And he gets it!"

Stella launched herself at Joe. She was livid.

"Of *course* I'm mad at you!" she yelled, smacking him upside the head with his own ridiculous-looking hat. "How *dare* you butt into my personal life! My personal life is none of your business! On the door to my personal life, it says KEEP OUT, JOE!"

She gave him one last smack with the hat. Joe cringed.

"If you're done hitting me, can I please put

on my real clothes now?" he asked meekly. "I'm sorry!"

Stella glanced at Nick and Kevin. "I don't know," she said. "Do you think he's learned his lesson?"

Before Joe's brothers could answer, the door opened. The Big Man's big head poked in.

"They're ready, guys," the Big Man said in his big, gruff voice. He blinked and stared at Joe. "Excuse me, ma'am," he added politely. "Where's Joe?"

Mr. Lucas entered the dressing room a moment later. He took one look at Joe and said, "Okay. *What* is going on?"

Joe and Stella pointed at each other and immediately began speaking at the same time. "She made me wear this! She got some idea in her head that I ruined her date—" Joe began.

"The only reason he's wearing that outfit is because—" Stella was saying.

"—when I couldn't care less about some jock she drags to the movies—" Joe continued.

"—he purposely ruined my date. Not to mention all the outfits I put together—" Stella went on.

Mr. Lucas had heard enough. He gave a very loud, very shrill whistle and Joe and Stella fell silent. Then Mr. Lucas turned to Kevin and Nick.

"Did you two know anything about this?" he asked.

"About what?" Kevin asked, feigning confusion.

"Not a thing," Nick said innocently.

Stella gasped at their betrayal.

"Okay, this is what's going to happen," Mr. Lucas said, turning back to Joe. "We will go out there as is and you will meet the prime minister. If feathers get ruffled, I'll make sure to smooth them out," he said confidently. "Let's go." He began to march out and everyone followed him. But when he got to the door, he turned to Joe again. "At least take off the hat," he said.

"No!" Stella protested. "You'll ruin the whole look!"

Joe looked at his dad. "I hate to say it, but

she has a point," he admitted.

The prime minister was just another guy, right? Joe mused. Maybe he'd have a sense of humor about this. Or maybe Joe really was just cool enough to pull off this look. All he could do at this point was try. . . .

Joe straightened his shoulders and shuffled into line with his brothers. A British official met them and led them down a hall, but not before eyeing Joe doubtfully. Joe tried not to pay any attention to that.

"Thank you, Prime Minister," Kevin muttered under his breath nearby. He'd been practicing all morning. "Thank you, Prime Minister . . ."

"Are we all ready?" the embassy official asked in his crisp British accent. Then he cleared his throat and continued loudly, "Ladies and gentlemen, Her Majesty, the Queen!"

Kevin's jaw dropped. "Her *what* the *who*?" he cried.

Nick leaned toward the official. "What happened to the Prime Minister?" he hissed.

"The Prime Minister overdid it at the Bangers and Mash Festival this morning," the official replied. "Her Majesty graciously interrupted her tour of the Academy of Lovable Cockney Street Urchins to present you with your commendation."

There was a commotion by the doorway. A conservative coif topped with a tasteful pink hat appeared.

Watching from the dressing-room doorway, Stella was in a full-on panic. Talk about a fashion disaster!

"Joe!" she hissed. "Get out of there! You can't be dressed like that in front of a queen!"

"Too late," Joe hissed back. "The redcoats are coming!"

The Queen stepped into the room. She glided regally over to the brothers. "In recognition of your efforts on behalf of the Royal Children's Hospital," she said in a cultured and regal voice, "we present to you these commendations of merit."

Flashes popped as the photographer snapped

picture after picture. The Queen made her way—slowly, regally—down the line. She paused in front of each brother to hand over a scroll and shake hands.

When Joe's turn came, he managed to stammer a thank you. He even bowed. Wasn't that what you were supposed to do when meeting royalty? He wasn't sure, but he figured at least it would hide the goofy sunglasses. He stayed down as the Queen finished and turned away.

Beside him, Kevin was still bowing, too. "Hey!" Kevin whispered to Joe while they were still both bent over. "It's all good. She didn't even notice what you're wearing."

That made Joe feel a little better. He stood up—just in time to see the Queen stop and turn back toward them.

"Oh, we noticed," she said in her regal voice.

Joe winced. Darn that Kevin and his loud whispers!

"It's . . . it's just kind of a joke," he stammered.

The Queen sniffed. "We are not amused."

With that, she turned away again and swept out of the room.

Kevin elbowed Joe. "If she throws you into her dungeon, can I have your new guitar?"

CHAPTER EIGHT

A few days later, Stella and the guys were cruising the hall at school. They were passing around the latest issue of *News Report* magazine. Joe was on the cover, dressed in the outfit he'd worn to meet the Queen. The headline blared: ROCK 'N' ROLL ROYALTY!

Joe stared at the ridiculous picture. "I can never show my face in public again," he moaned.

"No! Everyone says the ceremony was a hit,"

Stella said. "People love that JONAS doesn't take itself too seriously."

"I know," Kevin agreed. "Look at this fan letter I just got." He pulled out a folded piece of paper, flipped it open, and started to read: "'The silkworm, native to many regions of China, starts his day . . .'"

He stopped reading and blinked in confusion. That wasn't how he remembered the fan letter starting.

Then his eyes widened. "Uh-oh," he cried. "This is my biology report! I must've turned that fan letter in to Mrs. Kapp. That won't get me any better than a B-plus!"

Meanwhile, in a classroom elsewhere in the building, biology teacher Mrs. Kapp stared down at a sheet of paper. It was covered in little drawings of hearts. Puzzling. She appreciated Kevin Lucas's attempt to study something as complex as the human heart, but where was the rest of the report?

Back in the hallway, Kevin had just taken off in

the direction of the biology room. Joe watched him go, then turned to Stella.

"Stella," he said earnestly, "I hope you know I'm sorry about spoiling your date with Van Dyke. I don't know what I was thinking. I know I've said I'm sorry about four hundred times, but . . . I really am sorry."

"Let's make a deal," Stella replied. "From now on, we stay out of each other's personal lives."

Joe shrugged. For some reason, the suggestion left him feeling a little bummed out. Still, the most important thing was to make Stella happy.

"If that's what you want," he said. It felt a little weird to promise something like that. But what else could he do?

Stella shot him a look. "Isn't that what *you* want?"

"Of course that's what I want."

"Me, too," Stella said quickly. "What I want. That."

To cover her own weird feeling—where had that weird feeling come from, anyway?—she stuck out her hand. Joe was Joe. Her buddy, her pal. Joe took her hand, automatically sliding into their old secret handshake from when they were kids. It involved pinkies, elbows, knees, and even hips. The handshake was so familiar that it chased away the weird feelings. Most of them, anyway.

"Hey, guess what I just heard?" Nick said to Joe when the two were finished. "You know that girl—"

Joe cut him off. "The really hot one we saw in the cafeteria?" he asked, guessing exactly which girl Nick meant. "In the red dress and headband with the little daisies on her nails ordering the banana-nut muffin?"

"They were sunflowers on her nails," Nick corrected. "Anyway, I overheard her telling her friend that she's going to ask you out for Saturday."

Stella blinked slowly. The handshake hadn't

completely worked. The weird feeling was back.

"Saturday night, huh?" Joe said, his expression brightening.

"Not *this* Saturday?" Stella blurted out.

"Why not?" Joe shrugged. "I'm free."

Stella waved the copy of *News Report* in front of his face. "Did you *not* see this?" she demanded. "We have a fashion emergency here. I can't have people thinking this is the look I designed for you. My rep would be ruined!"

Just then Van Dyke appeared at the end of the hallway. He was dressed in the same ridiculous outfit Joe had worn for the Queen. Down to every last sequin.

"Hey, Stells," he said, hurrying over. "Free for a movie Saturday? Then I thought we could hit the mall and let everyone check out my new look." He posed and preened. The fluorescent hallway lights made his sequins shimmer.

"Um . . ." Stella said, suddenly a lot less into Van Dyke.

"Great idea!" Joe put in brightly, a mischievous

smile on his face. "We can double date. See you Saturday!"

Turning, he headed to class. Nick and Joe traded knowing smiles. One thing was for sure. Life on tour wasn't where all the drama happened!

PART ONE

Stella Malone, JONAS's stylist and best friend, welcomes the boys back from being on tour.

Joe Lucas discovers at least one downside to going on tour—unpacking!

Joe can't stop thinking about Stella and Van Dyke's date!

Kevin Lucas tries to calm down Stella after she learns of Joe's wardrobe disaster.

Talk about a fashion faux pas! Joe offends the Queen of England with his outfit.

"From now on, we stay out of each other's personal lives," Stella tells Joe.

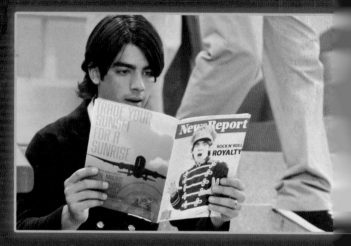

Joe is front-page news! He reads up on his "fashion disaster."

Stella can't believe her eyes. Van Dyke is wearing the same ridiculous outfit

PART TWO

Nick Lucas has a confession to make: he's crushing . . . again.

Nick daydreams about his crush, Penny.

Macy Misa can't believe it! She is wearing
the exact jacket that Joe will wear.

Macy is getting a little tired of being
Stella's mannequin.

"Why is there sheet music in the shower?"
Mr. Lucas asks Nick.

Nick tries to have a heart-to-heart
with Penny.

Nick lets Penny record music in the JONAS studio—even after she stole his song.

Penny tells Nick she has broken up with her boyfriend. "So . . . then the song is available?" Nick asks hopefully.

PART
TWO

CHAPTER ONE

"Do you see what I see?" Joe Lucas asked his brother Kevin.

Kevin wasn't sure. He looked around. The two of them were walking past the glass atrium at the center of their school, the Horace Mantis Academy. Kevin glanced up through the atrium's glass ceiling at the sky outside. Aha!

"A cloud in the shape of a rabbit!" he exclaimed. He loved this game. "Cute!"

Joe shook his head. "Lower."

Kevin looked lower. This time he scanned the floor of the atrium. Aha! "A rabbit in the shape of a cloud! Even cuter!" he exclaimed.

"Higher," Joe said.

Kevin looked a bit higher and . . . saw his other brother sitting on the steps at the far side of the atrium. Aha!

"Nick with a goofy smile on his face," he said. Then he did a double take and repeated, "Nick with a goofy smile on his face?"

Joe nodded, staring. "Now *that's* something you don't see every day."

That was true. The three Lucas brothers were in a supersuccessful band called JONAS. And every JONAS fan out there knew that Nick was not a goofy-smile type of guy. Kevin, definitely. Joe, maybe. But Nick? No way. He was more the intense, brooding type. When he smiled, that smile was usually deep. Soulful. Sensitive. In other words, definitely *not* goofy.

Over on the stairs, Nick didn't even notice

his brothers looking at him from across the way. All his attention was on the girl with long blond hair sitting next to him. That was another thing Joe and Kevin didn't see every day. Nick? And a girl?

The girl's name was Penny, and Nick knew he'd never met anyone like her.

"Are you kidding?" Penny was exclaiming, her adorable eyes dancing. "I *love* golf! My dad taught me. You're into it, too?"

"It's, like, my favorite sport," Nick replied. "Not a lot of people appreciate golf. What's your favorite part of the game?"

"Hitting the ball through the clown's mouth and watching it come out his pants," Penny said sincerely.

Nick laughed. Penny did, too. Then they just sort of sat there and smiled at each other for a while.

Nick was pretty sure he'd be happy to sit there and gaze into her face for the rest of the day. Possibly even the rest of the week.

Finally the bell rang, and they had to part ways. Nick stood up, reluctant to say good-bye. But he was determined to see Penny again—as soon as possible.

As she hurried off to class, Nick wandered over to his locker. There he found Joe and Kevin waiting for him.

"Hey, guys," Nick said cheerfully. He was so happy, in fact, he didn't notice the intense looks on his brothers' faces.

"So, what's her name?" Joe demanded.

"What's whose name?" Nick asked, playing coy. He liked to keep things close to the chest. He wasn't much of a sharer. Kevin and Joe were the sharers.

Joe was not going to let up. He crossed his arms. "The girl you're crushin' on." He waited for an answer.

"'Crushin'?'" Nick echoed. "What are you, eleven?" Then he shrugged, playing it cool. "I think she said her name was Jenny or Penny. Or something."

Kevin sighed and glanced at Joe. They weren't buying the cool act. "Here we go again," Kevin said.

"What are you talking about?" Nick said, raising an eyebrow.

"You always fall too hard, too fast." Joe shook his head sadly. "You meet a girl and it's like boom—instant love. Then it's boom—you get dumped. Then it's boom—broken heart. And me and Kevin have to pick up the pieces."

Kevin peered down at the floor. "Oh, look. There's Nick's heart." He bent over and pretended to pick up small pieces of something from the floor.

"That's happened, like, one time," Nick said, protesting.

Joe and Kevin shook their heads. "Six times," they corrected in unison.

"Well, don't worry." Nick turned to his locker. "I'm taking it nice and slooooooooow."

He opened the locker. But he made sure his brothers couldn't see inside. So what if there were pictures of Penny taped up on the door? That didn't mean he wasn't planning on taking things nice and slow, just like he'd told them. . . .

CHAPTER TWO

In another part of Horace Mantis, Stella Malone and her friend Macy Misa were doing some serious work. Stella opened her locker. It was crammed full of superfashionable clothes. Not only was she a student, she happened to be friend of and head stylist for JONAS. The guys and their clothes were always on her mind. Surveying the small but fabulous collection, she plucked out a snazzy-looking jacket and handed it to Macy.

Macy obediently took the jacket. She was more of a jock than a fashionista herself. But she was always happy to help her friend exercise her flawless sense of style.

"So why am I putting this on?" she asked.

"It's going to be Joe's," Stella said. "And I want to—"

Macy's loud gasp cut her off. "*Joe's* going to wear this?" she demanded, trembling.

"Yeah," Stella said, "and I want to see if—"

Once again, she didn't get to finish. Macy was clutching the jacket, her eyes looking sort of spacey and glazed over.

"Joe's going to put his arms through these sleeves . . ." Macy murmured reverently. She poked her own arms through the sleeves. "And his hands are going to come out these holes." She watched in awe as her own hands appeared at the cuffs. She held them up and stared at them. "These will be Joe's hands!" She placed her hands on her own cheeks. Her eyes fluttered shut.

"Macy," Stella said. "Macy?" She sighed. She

should have known better. Macy was the number one JONAS fan in school. Possibly in the universe. It was sometimes way too easy for Stella to forget that not everyone had been best buds with the Lucas brothers practically since birth. Not everyone was their stylist who saw them just about every day, either. No, not everyone. And especially not Macy.

Finally Macy blinked, snapping out of her reverie. "How long was I out?" she asked Stella sheepishly.

Stella decided to let the question pass. She had exciting news. "So," she said, "you know how crazed fans sometimes go after Kevin, Joe, or Nick and rip and tear their clothes to get a souvenir?"

Macy's cheeks went pink. "I couldn't help it!" she blurted out. "Nick was standing so close. So I reached through the crowd, grabbed his red shirt, and—"

"That was *you*?" Stella cried.

Macy reached into her backpack and pulled

71

out a scrap of red fabric. She ducked her head and rubbed it on her cheek. Then she sighed and handed it to Stella.

Stella grabbed it and surveyed it. "You see?" she exclaimed. "A perfectly good shirt—ruined! That's why I created a new line of clothing I call Stelcro. Patent pending. Now, when an overly excited fan grabs one of the guys' jackets, the sleeve will break away."

She reached over and yanked at one of the sleeves on the jacket Macy was wearing. Macy let out a startled yelp as it peeled away with a loud ripping sound.

"Then, instead of throwing out a beautiful and expensive garment"—she paused and glared briefly at Macy—"all I have to do is replace the sleeve."

Leaning over, she stuck the sleeve over Macy's bare arm and pushed it back into place. Then she reattached it to the body of the jacket and stepped away, looking pleased.

"Voila!" she said. "Less work for Stella."

Macy smiled, stroking the sleeve. "More sleeve for Macy!"

Just then something over by the atrium caught Stella's eye. She glanced that way and lifted her eyebrows in surprise. "Do you see what I see?" she asked.

Macy looked that way, too. "Weird," she said. "That guy looks just like Nick. Except he's smiling."

"It *is* Nick," Stella said. She recognized that particularly sappy look on Nick's face. "And he's more than smiling—he's smitten." A smile crept across her face. "And just when my gossip tank was running on empty . . ."

CHAPTER THREE

Nick leaned closer to Penny. He couldn't take his eyes off her. She'd looked amazing enough before. Now that she was sitting there with a guitar in her hands, she looked totally incredible!

The two of them were hanging out, getting to know each other better. Nick couldn't believe how easy it was to talk to Penny. Right now they were telling each other stories about when they were younger. "I've got a better one," Nick told her with a smile. "When I was little, my nickname was Nickel."

Penny laughed, strumming softly on the guitar. "No way! A Penny and a Nickel!"

"It's got to be fate." Nick glanced at the guitar. "And how cool is it that you love golf *and* play guitar?"

"I can't believe I'm even playing in front of you," Penny said, suddenly shy. After all, he was a bona fide rock star and she was just a beginner!

"You sound great."

"I have my first real performance on Friday night at CBDB's," she said. "Want to come?"

"I'm there," Nick said enthusiastically.

Penny gulped and smiled. Now she wasn't just shy, she was nervous, too.

Nick couldn't believe it. Penny was even more adorable when she was nervous!

"The trick is to look bored while you're playing," he advised. "Then the audience thinks you really know what you're doing."

He stood up and reached for her guitar. Then he sort of slouched, his eyes half closed, and strummed a few chords.

Penny laughed. "And what's the trick to recording my first demo?" she teased.

"To do it in our studio," Nick replied as though that were the most obvious answer in the world.

Penny grew wide-eyed. Record a demo at a real studio—the *JONAS* studio? She could hardly believe her ears. "Are you serious?" she asked.

"Of course," Nick said. "Just read the fan magazines. I'm the 'serious' one."

Penny laughed. Then she leaped to her feet and flung her arms around Nick to thank him. She couldn't believe how awesome he was being—especially since they'd just met!

Nick hugged her back.

In the hallway just outside the atrium, Joe and Kevin were watching. "Look at them, all cozy," Joe commented. He had a gleam in his eye.

"It would be so wrong to butt in," Kevin said with a smirk.

The two of them traded a look. Then they headed into the atrium.

"Nick!" Kevin exclaimed in mock surprise when they got closer.

"Didn't see you out here," Joe added casually.

Nick frowned at them. "Really?" he said, unconvinced. "Because this whole thing's glass, and we're the only two people here."

Kevin ignored him. "Ah, this must be Penny," he said. "We've heard so much about you."

"No, they haven't," Nick told Penny hastily.

"All Captain McHappy here does is talk about how wonderful you are," Joe said.

"No, I don't," Nick protested.

"It's nonstop," Joe added.

"No, it's not!" Nick was really getting irritated now. Did his brothers have to butt in on everything he did? Why couldn't they just leave him alone?

Luckily, Penny didn't seem to mind too

much. She was smiling at Joe and Kevin.

She is such a nice, sweet person that she probably doesn't even notice what huge pains they are being, Nick thought with adoration. Still, he wasn't taking any chances. "I apologize for their juvenile behavior," he told her.

"Hey!" Kevin protested. "I can apologize for my own juvenile behavior, thank you very much."

Just then, Stella hurried into the atrium. She made a beeline for them.

"Are these clowns bothering you?" she asked Nick and Penny.

"No," Kevin and Joe chorused.

"Yes," Nick snapped at the same time.

Stella turned to face Kevin and Joe, who were attempting to look innocent—and failing. "How about leaving the guy alone?" she suggested in her no-nonsense way. "He's hangin' with a friend. I think he deserves a little privacy."

Kevin shrugged and glanced at Nick. "See you back home, Captain McHappy."

"Hey," Joe said, "*I* came up with that!"

They wandered off, still arguing. Nick heaved a sigh of relief, and ran a hand through his curly hair. "Thanks, Stella," he said when Joe and Kevin had gone.

Stella smiled. Nick waited for her to leave, too. She didn't.

Instead, she plopped down right next to Penny. "I want to know everything," she declared. "Don't leave anything out. Nothing's too personal. Start at the beginning. Where did you two meet?"

"Stella!" Nick exclaimed through clenched teeth.

Apparently, this wasn't a good time for girl talk. Stella shrugged. Never mind—she could wait to grill Penny later.

Jumping to her feet, Stella waved good-bye. "Well, it was great meeting you!" she told Penny cheerfully.

"You, too," Penny replied.

With one last cheery wave, Stella hurried off.

Nick sighed with relief, then gave Penny an apologetic shrug.

She just smiled in return, totally unbothered. Nick smiled back, feeling himself relax.

Yeah, he thought. *This* is more like it.

CHAPTER FOUR

Spotting Stella in the hallway, Macy hurried over. She was walking a little funny and her shoulders looked oddly boxy.

"I liked the jacket better," she told Stella, glancing down at the shirt she was wearing. It was another Stella original. "This feels a little stiff."

Stella nodded thoughtfully, examining the shirt with a critical eye. So far Stelcro was looking like a success, but that didn't mean there weren't a few wrinkles left to iron out in the various designs.

"I'm still working on a softer thread for the seams," she explained to Macy. "Okay, now pretend you're one of the JONAS guys, and—"

Once again, she wasn't able to finish her sentence. "Oh!" Macy interrupted with a squeak of excitement. "Which one should I be? I'll be Joe. He's so cool! Just the way he walks . . ."

She strutted down the hallway . . . and promptly tripped.

"Or maybe Kevin," she said. "He's so out there and wild!"

She started imitating Kevin, jumping around and making crazy faces as she tore up the stage on air guitar. Stella just sighed.

"Or Nick!" Macy cried, her voice getting even louder. "With all that intensity!"

She stopped moving and just stood there, an intense expression on her face.

Stella shook her head. "What do you do, follow them around all day?"

"No, of course not!" Macy protested quickly. Then she added, "Why? Do they see me?"

Stella decided it was time to move on. This kind of one-sided conversation could go on all day if she wasn't careful. "Okay," she said briskly, "so now *you're* a JONAS and *I'm* a crazed fan." She took a deep breath and let out a scream. "Aaaah! It's JONAS! It's JONAS!"

She grabbed at the shirt Macy was wearing, yanking on one sleeve as hard as she could. Fabric came away in her hand.

But wait. Wasn't that a little *too much* fabric? Stella blinked at the shirt she was holding. The *entire* shirt. Then she glanced up at Macy. She did not look happy.

Macy let out a shriek of embarrassment. Stella quickly grabbed the extra blazer she carried at all times and handed it to her friend.

"This is why we test these things," she muttered. Then she glanced at some passing students who were giving them interesting looks. Maybe school wasn't the *best* place for testing Stelcro. "Nothing to see here!"

Meanwhile Joe and Kevin were at their lockers trying to have a conversation. It wasn't easy. They had to raise their voices to talk to each other. That's because the whir of a blender coming from inside one of the lockers was doing its best to drown them out. Still, they weren't going to let the sound get in the way of their *very* important conversation.

"Okay, I'm thinking of someone," Joe said. "Twenty questions. Go."

Kevin nodded eagerly. This was one of his favorite games.

"Is it someone famous?" he asked.

"Yes," Joe confirmed.

"Is it me?" Kevin guessed.

"No."

"Is it Will Smith?"

Joe looked impressed. "Man, you're good!"

Just then, the whir of the blender stopped. Kevin opened his locker and took out two smoothies. He handed one to Joe.

84

"One banana smoothie with an immunity boost," he announced.

"Thanks." Joe sipped his smoothie. Ah—so refreshing!

"Okay, now *I'm* thinking of something," Kevin said, continuing the game. "It's an animal."

"An otter that plays the trumpet?" Joe said, giving it his best guess.

Kevin sighed and smiled. "We just know each other too well."

Joe glanced over his shoulder. "Hey, take a look," he said.

Kevin looked in the direction of Joe's gaze. Penny was sitting on a bench in the atrium—alone.

"It's Penny, and there's no sign of Nick," Kevin said in surprise. "Maybe he really is taking it slow this time."

As if on cue, Nick came into view. He was racing down the hall, dodging students and teachers like a linebacker and clutching his guitar. From the look on his face, there was no doubt where—or to whom—he was racing.

"Coming through!" he cried breathlessly. "Excuse me. Sorry."

Together, Kevin and Joe stepped out in front of him. Nick had no choice. He came to a screeching halt.

"Want to play twenty questions?" Joe asked him.

Nick frowned impatiently, glancing toward the atrium. "Not now."

Joe wasn't taking no for an answer. "I'm thinking of someone," he insisted.

"I'll go!" Kevin jumped in. "Is it a girl? Is Nick moving too fast with her? Does her name rhyme with Flenny?"

"Yes! Yes! And yes," Joe said in a praising tone.

"Guys, lay off!" Nick protested. "Just because Penny plays like an angel, smiles like an angel, and makes me feel like I'm in heaven, that doesn't mean I'm moving too fast."

He didn't wait around to hear their response.

86

Dodging around them, he raced into the atrium.

His brothers watched him go. Then Kevin turned to Joe. "You *were* thinking Penny, right?" he asked.

CHAPTER FIVE

Penny was sitting on "their" bench playing her guitar when Nick rushed up. She smiled at him.

"Hey there, you," she greeted.

Okay, Nick thought. Play it cool. Don't move too fast—

"I wrote you a song!" he blurted out.

Then he gulped, feeling foolish. He'd meant to be a little cooler about it.

"What?" Penny looked confused.

"I can't wait to play it for you," he said, lifting his guitar. "Want to hear it?"

"Are you kidding?" Penny exclaimed. She couldn't believe this was happening.

Nick grinned. Then he started to play the opening chords of his song. He had worked on it all morning. It was one of the best ones he'd ever written, and that was all thanks to Penny. She was his new inspiration.

He sang, pouring everything he had into the song. His eyes drifted shut, and he could almost imagine Penny transforming into a real angel, complete with enormous, fluffy white wings. True, those huge wings could be a little inconvenient in the crowded school hallways. Might even cause a few accidents. But so what? Nick banished those goofy thoughts and opened his eyes.

Penny was gazing up at him in awe. He sat down beside her to finish the song, singing directly to her.

When he was done, she clasped her hands together. "Wow!" she breathed. "That was—that was beautiful! You wrote that for *me*?"

Nick nodded. "I hope that's okay," he said, suddenly feeling a little bashful. It was one thing to perform in front of thousands of adoring fans as part of JONAS. But this felt different. A whole lot more personal. And a whole lot scarier. But one look at Penny's beaming face reassured him.

"Are you kidding?" she cried. "It's the coolest thing ever! No one's ever written a song for me. Let alone a rock star!"

Nick let out a big sigh of relief. Then he smiled.

"You have a great smile," Penny told him, gushing happily.

"Shh," Nick joked. "You'll ruin my image."

"Can you teach it to me?" Penny begged.

Nick was a little surprised by the question. He had never been asked that before. "It's nothing, really," he said. "You just turn up the corners of your mouth, and—"

Penny laughed. "The *song*! I want to learn the song."

That made Nick smile even more. If she wanted to learn the song, that must mean she *really* liked it! He started strumming his guitar again, slower this time, to give her a chance to follow the chords. . . .

CHAPTER SIX

That night at the renovated firehouse where the Lucas family lived, Nick stood in front of the Stellavator touch-screen on the wall. The Stellavator was one of Stella's greatest achievements. The boys just put in the details of an event, and the Stellavator picked out the perfect outfit. At the moment, Nick was frozen in fear.

Joe and Kevin came in and saw him. They exchanged glances.

"Are you still trying to figure out what to wear to your girlfriend's show?" Joe asked Nick.

"She's not my girlfriend," Nick mumbled, still focused on the Stellavator.

Kevin rolled his eyes. "Obviously you're crazy about this girl."

Joe nodded wisely. "And just a little nervous about whether she likes you, too," he added.

Nick shot them an annoyed look. "I'm not nervous."

"Oh, really?" Joe said. He shot a look at Nick's feet.

Nick looked down. Oops. He was wearing one boot and one sneaker.

"It's a look Stella came up with," he said quickly, trying to cover. Then he hesitated. "Uh, but don't tell Stella."

"Bro, we're worried you're doing that falling-hard-and-fast thing again," Kevin said.

"I'm not!" Nick argued.

"Dude!" Joe exclaimed. "You wrote her a song!"

Nick winced. Busted! "How did you know?"

Joe glanced around the loft and shrugged. "There's sheet music everywhere."

Kevin leaned over and grabbed a few pages of sheet music off the floor. "'Burnin' Up Over Penny,'" he read aloud. "'Penny Got Me Goin' Crazy.'"

Before he could go on, their father hurried in. Mr. Lucas was wearing a JONAS bathrobe, slippers, and shower cap. He waved a handful of sopping wet papers at them.

"Why is there sheet music in the shower?" he asked.

"Sorry," Nick said.

Mr. Lucas read the wet music he was holding. "'S.O.S. Penny.' 'When You Look Me in the Eyes, Penny.'" He glanced up with a knowing smile. "Is someone too much in love again?"

"I'm not in love," Nick insisted. "And would everybody please stop saying 'again'? It happened a couple of times!"

"Six times," Mr. Lucas clarified. He stepped forward, as if about to impart a great piece of wisdom. "I'll let you in on a little secret. Your mom was the twenty-third love of my life."

Nick, Joe, and Kevin were all shocked. No way! Their parents were the perfect couple. At least for a couple of old people. They were totally meant for each other—everyone said so. And they'd been together practically forever— since they were both, like, Frankie's age.

"Yeah," Mr. Lucas said. "I was walking down the aisle on the school bus. I saw twenty-two other girls before I got to your mom." He pumped his arm triumphantly. "Gotcha!" he cried with a laugh. "But seriously, Nick. I'm here for you if that little heart of yours breaks again."

Nick glowered at him. Mr. Lucas raised his hands in defense.

"Not *again*," he amended. "For the first time. Ever."

"It's cool," Kevin told their father. "Me and Joe got it covered."

Their dad shrugged. Then he wandered out, wringing the sheet music he was holding.

Once he was gone, Nick glanced at his brothers. "Just for the record," he said, "I went with 'Give Love a Try.'" He didn't want his brothers to think *all* his songs had Penny's name in the title.

"So how about we go with you to Penny's show tonight?" Joe suggested. "You know, just for support."

"No," Nick said quickly. "If you guys go it'll draw too much attention. Everyone will be looking at JONAS instead of watching Penny."

Kevin shrugged. "So we'll go low-key."

Nick gulped nervously. "*Actual* low-key?" he asked. "Or *your* version of low-key?"

CHAPTER SEVEN

Nick found out the answer to that question all too soon.

Penny's gig was being held at a dimly lit venue. When they arrived, Nick quickly found a seat at a table near the back. He was wearing a baseball cap and sunglasses. Definitely low-key. Even the biggest JONAS fan would have to look twice to recognize him.

Then there was Joe. Baseball cap? That would

be too easy! Instead, he'd gone with a large handlebar mustache and a monocle.

Kevin, on the other hand, had chosen a more . . . mature look. He was dressed in a white suit and a floppy tie, with flowing locks of snow white hair and a matching mustache.

"You see?" Kevin told Nick when he and Joe had arrived. "Nobody knows JONAS is even in the house."

Nick couldn't believe his brothers' outfits. No, scratch that—actually, he *could* believe them. It was fairly typical.

"Seriously," he said to Kevin, "how did you get to be the oldest?"

"I'm not that old," Kevin replied. Silly Nick, he thought. He doesn't get it's a disguise. He leaned closer and lowered his voice, pointing to his flowing white hair. "It's a wig."

Joe wasn't paying attention to his brothers. He was wriggling around in his seat like a toddler who couldn't sit still.

"What's up with you?" Nick asked him.

"Stella got me to test a pair of her new Stelcro pants," Joe said. "They itch like crazy!"

Just then, Penny walked onstage. She was holding her guitar and looking nervous but excited.

Nick started clapping as hard as he could. Everyone else in the club applauded, too. Penny smiled.

"Thank you," she said. Then she took a deep breath. "I'd like to start off this set with my newest song. It's called 'Give Love a Try.' Hope you like it!"

She started to play. As the music filled the room, Nick just sat there, stunned.

"Isn't that the song Nick wrote?" Joe asked Kevin when Penny reached the chorus.

Kevin didn't bother to answer. "Dude!" he whispered to Nick. "Your girlfriend is *stealing* your song!"

Nick bit his lip. He didn't need Kevin to tell him that. It was all too clear. But why would Penny do this? There had to be an explanation.

99

"I wrote that song for her," he whispered back to Kevin, playing it cool. "She can do what she wants with it." Then he added, "And she's *not* my girlfriend."

A few notes later, Penny suddenly stopped singing and playing. "I completely forgot," she said, still sounding nervous. "I want to dedicate this song to the coolest, grooviest, sweetest guy on the planet."

Nick smiled. That was more like it! Maybe it had just been a big misunderstanding!

"A guy who has a heart filled with music," Penny went on.

Now Nick was starting to feel sort of self-conscious. It was amazing that she wanted to thank him for the song this way, but if she didn't watch it she was going to blow his cover. . . .

"My soul mate," Penny continued, "Jimmy!"

Jimmy? Wait, was this her way of not blowing Nick's cover or something? Or was it a new pet name she'd forgotten to tell him about? For a second Nick was confused.

Then the truth hit him like a punch in the gut. He glanced around the room. At a table nearby, a cool-looking guy around his own age was waving happily at Penny. The dude was even wearing a homemade T-shirt that read: I ♥ PENNY. It had to be Jimmy.

Penny smiled adoringly at Jimmy. Then she started singing Nick's song again.

Joe leaned in to Nick. "Dude, your girlfriend has a boyfriend," he said.

Nick scowled at him. "She's not my girlfriend!" he hissed. He shot a look at Penny onstage, then looked back at his brothers. "Can we just go?"

"Yeah, sure," Joe said sympathetically.

"Whatever you want," Kevin added.

Nick got up and headed for the door, not looking back. He didn't want to see Penny right now. And he *especially* didn't want to see Jimmy— or his shirt.

Kevin stood up to follow. Then he glanced back at Joe. He was stopped in a sort of half-standing, half-sitting position.

"Uh-oh," Joe whispered. "I think I put the Stelcro jeans on inside out."

"How do you know?" Kevin asked.

"Just a feeling."

Joe stood up the rest of the way. The chair came with him. It was stuck to his butt!

But Joe didn't panic. As a member of JONAS, he'd had to cover for stuff that went wrong onstage plenty of times. He knew how to play it cool. He just strolled out of the club—the chair following right behind him.

CHAPTER EIGHT

The next morning, Nick sat alone on the atrium bench. He was strumming his guitar, playing a sad instrumental version of "Give Love a Try." The song had been running through his head that way all night—ever since he'd watched Penny dedicate it to Jimmy. Her boyfriend.

Through the glass, Kevin and Joe watched their brother. They exchanged a curious look as they saw Penny rush into the atrium. She looked happy and excited. Kevin and Joe pressed their ears against the glass to try and hear everything.

"What happened to you last night?" Penny asked breathlessly, skidding to a stop in front of Nick.

Nick glanced up. It was hard not to smile at the sight of Penny. But he managed. "I was in the back, kind of on the down-low, and Joe was wearing his pants inside out. . . ." He shrugged. "It's a long story."

"So what did you think?" Penny asked. "Your opinion means a lot to me."

Nick took a deep breath. "Actually, I was kind of surprised to hear you sing 'Give Love a Try,'" he admitted.

Penny looked surprised. "But you wrote it for me to sing, right?"

Suddenly Nick felt like one of those cartoon characters. The ones who catch on to something and a little lightbulb sparks on over their heads.

"Oh . . ." he began.

"Isn't that why you wrote it?" Penny's excited

expression was fading. She was starting to look worried.

Nick sighed. This was all his fault. It might have been his heart on the line but . . . "Yeah," he said quickly. "That's why I wrote it. I wrote it for you . . . to sing."

Penny still looked anxious. "You hated it!" she cried. "I feel awful!"

"Are you kidding?" Nick said. "You were awesome! And to hear you sing it to Jimmy, who apparently is your boyfriend, that was, uh, magical." Magical? Nick wanted to scream. What was he saying? Why was he being nice?

"Oh, I'm so relieved!" Penny cried, the worry disappearing from her eyes. She leaned over, gave Nick a quick kiss on the cheek, and then rushed off.

A second later, Kevin and Joe rushed in. "How did it go?" Joe asked. "We couldn't hear a thing."

"There was nothing to hear," Nick said.

"Nick, it's us," Kevin said. "We're here to pick up the pieces of your broken heart." He held up a

105

trash spike and a plastic bag. The bag had a picture of a broken heart on it.

Nick rolled his eyes. "My heart is totally intact." He gave a shrug. "We talked it all out. Big misunderstanding. Since Penny's already with Johnny—"

"Jimmy," Joe corrected helpfully.

"Whatever," Nick said. "She and I are just going to be friends."

"Really?" Kevin sounded suspicious.

"Everything's cool," Nick assured him. "I told you I wasn't moving too fast."

Kevin and Joe both shrugged. Nick certainly wasn't *acting* like a dude with a broken heart.

"I guess we had this one wrong," Joe said.

Nick nodded. "You sure did."

"Looks like our little Nickel is growing up," Kevin added.

"He sure is," Nick agreed, trying not to tear up. Nickel. Penny. It was all so fresh.

Just then Penny hurried back into the atrium. "I almost forgot," she said to Nick. "Remember when you said I could record a demo in your studio?"

"Yeah," Nick said weakly, careful not to make eye contact with his brothers. He could only imagine what they were thinking.

Penny beamed at him. "What do you think about me recording 'Give Love a Try'?"

"Uh . . ."

It was bad enough that Penny had misunderstood why he'd written her that song. Now she wanted to record it in his studio? But what could he do? He couldn't admit his true feelings after working so hard to cover them up. Especially not in front of his brothers.

"Sure," Nick said as cheerfully as he could manage. "That's a great idea. I mean, I wrote it for you, right?"

"You are awesome!" Penny cried, throwing her arms around him.

"So totally awesome," Joe put in with a smirk. He jumped forward and hugged Nick, too.

They were so busy hugging, none of them

noticed Stella and Macy walking down the hallway outside. Well, not walking, exactly. Stella was dragging Macy down the hall by the leg of her jeans.

"Hey!" Macy protested. "Ouch! Stop!"

Stella kept yanking on the jeans. Her experiments with Stelcro weren't going too well at the moment. First she'd spent the entire morning detaching the first pair of prototype jeans from that chair Joe had stuck them to the night before. And now this?

"I don't get it," she said through gritted teeth. "The leg should tear right off!"

"Yeah," Macy cried, feeling her leg stretch under the force of Stella's iron grip. "It's going to if you don't stop!"

CHAPTER NINE

Later that day, inside the firehouse studio, Nick, Kevin, and Joe bustled around adjusting their recording equipment. Penny was there, too. She was sitting out of the way, tuning her guitar.

"Your brother writes amazing songs," she commented to Joe and Kevin.

Nick glanced over. "It's nothing," he said, still playing it casual. "I write songs all the time."

109

"It's true," Kevin agreed. "He can write a song before breakfast."

Joe nodded. "But we never use them 'cause they're always like 'My Stomach's Growling for Love' or 'I Want My Love Over Easy'—"

Nick cut him off. "Why don't you go into the booth so we can get a level?" he suggested to Penny.

She nodded eagerly and headed into the sound booth. After getting herself settled in, she started to play. Joe put on a pair of headphones to listen. Kevin stepped over to adjust the levels on the soundboard. Nick just stood there, distracted by Penny.

"So Nick," Kevin said, breaking into his thoughts, "how do you want to attack this?"

Nick snapped out of it. This was just a recording session with a hot new artist. Er, a *talented* new artist. Not hot. Nothing like that. He was a pro—he could handle this.

"Okay, first we'll lay down the backing track," Nick said briskly. "Then pick up the rhythm guitar, and then we'll do the lead vocals." He glanced at Penny inside the booth. Huh? Where had those enormous, fluffy white angel wings come from?

He blinked, shook his head, then looked again. No wings. Just Penny. Funny, perfect Penny . . .

"I can't do this," he blurted out.

Then he raced over and grabbed one of the fire poles. A second later he slid downstairs and out of sight.

Kevin and Nick exchanged a worried look before hurrying over and sliding down their own poles.

From inside the booth, Penny watched in confusion. Where were they going?

Kevin and Joe caught up with Nick in the kitchen. "Dude," Kevin said, "what's going on?"

"Nothing," Nick muttered, kicking at the ground.

"Come on." Joe took a step toward him. "It's us."

111

Nick shook his head. "You're going to make fun of me."

"Dude, we're your brothers," Kevin said.

Joe nodded. "We're going to make fun of you no matter what."

Nick had to admit Joe had a point. Besides, he couldn't hold in his real feelings any longer. Nick needed to talk. "I didn't take it slow with Penny," he blurted out. "I burned rubber and went like a hundred miles an hour." He paused and shot them a sheepish glance. "Man. I thought I was getting better at the romance thing."

"Nope," Kevin said.

"Not at all," Joe added.

"I made a total idiot out of myself!" Nick exclaimed. "How dumb can I be?"

"You're not dumb," Joe assured him. "You're just . . . really, really intense. Which is sad for you—but lucky for the band, 'cause we get great songs out of it."

"True." Oddly enough, Joe's words—which were somewhat harsh—made Nick feel a tiny bit better. But there was still one big problem. Penny. "So now what do I do?"

"Well, you can spend the rest of the year hiding in your locker," Kevin suggested helpfully.

"Or you can go back upstairs," Joe said, "record Penny's demo, and when you're done say 'it was nice working with you, see you at school.'"

Nick thought about it. Kevin's option was kind of tempting. "If I do the locker thing, would you guys bring me food?" he asked.

"Absolutely not," Joe said.

Kevin rolled his eyes. "What do I look like, a waiter?"

Nick sighed. He knew what he had to do. Squaring his shoulders, he headed for the stairs.

CHAPTER TEN

Up in the studio, Penny was waiting patiently. "Everything okay?" she asked as the three brothers entered.

"Yeah," Nick said in his playing-it-casual voice. "We were just . . ."

Then he cut himself off. No. He wasn't going to do that anymore. He wasn't going to pretend. It just wasn't worth it. . . .

"Look," he said in a more serious way. "I need

to tell you something. When I said I wrote this song for you, I didn't mean I wrote it for you. I meant I wrote it *for* you."

"I know," Penny said cheerfully. "And it's totally awesome that you—"

She stopped. Finally she heard what he was saying. *Really* heard it.

"Oh," she said softly.

"I guess I kind of got carried away in my head a little bit," Nick admitted. "I do that sometimes."

Penny couldn't believe it. All this time she'd been psyched that a member of JONAS was even interested in being her friend. Hanging out with her. Writing her songs and offering to help her record a demo. And now she was finding out he was actually interested in *more* than that? It was crazy!

"I feel terrible," she said. "I hope you don't think I led you on. I really like you, and when you said you wrote me a song . . ."

"No, no," Nick broke in. "It was all me."

115

Penny shot him a sympathetic look. "You kind of fall hard, huh?"

"That's what they tell me." Nick glanced at his brothers. "And tell me."

"No wonder you write such good songs," Penny said. She paused, biting her lip. Despite how nice Nick was being about this, she still felt pretty silly about what had happened. How could she have misunderstood everything so badly?

"I'll get my stuff and go," she said sadly.

Nick hesitated. He looked over again at Kevin and Joe. They nodded.

"Wait," Nick told Penny. "We should at least record the song."

Penny looked uncertain. "I can't sing it now that I know the truth about why you wrote it."

No matter how confusing it had all gotten, Nick couldn't let things end like this. After all, he was the sensitive one. Even if Penny couldn't be his angel, maybe they could still be friends.

"Won't Jimmy be disappointed?" he said. "You dedicated the song to him and stuff."

"Oh, I broke up with him," Penny said.

Nick blinked. "Why?"

"He didn't like the song," Penny replied. "And anyone who doesn't like an awesome song like this just doesn't get me."

She took a step toward Nick. He was still trying to take in what she was saying.

"So . . ." he said, "then the song is available?"

Penny smiled. "It's completely unattached."

Nick smiled back. "Come on," he said, reaching for her hand. "We have a demo to record."

And so they did. Joe and Kevin manned the board while Nick and Penny went into the booth together. And it turned out, "Give Love a Try" sounded even better as a duet.

THE END . . . well, not quite . . .

* * *

The next day at school, Kevin, Joe, and Nick stood in the hallway. They were all wearing super-stylish outfits, as usual. Stella was facing them, holding a clipboard. She surveyed her test subjects, feeling confident that this time her experiment would be a success.

"Okay," she said briskly. "Now the final test is to see if your average fan can tell which is the Stelcro garment."

Then she turned to Macy, who stood beside her. Macy looked a little excited. Okay, more than a little. It wasn't every day that she came face to face with all three of the JONAS guys at once. Well, actually, it was every school day, but still—she was practically quivering.

"Two of the guys are wearing regular clothes," Stella told her. "One is wearing Stelcro. I want you to see if you can tell which one is the—"

She didn't get to finish. Macy was unable to contain herself any longer. With a squeal of excitement, she leaped at Joe. Within seconds,

118

she'd torn away at his shirt, leaving him standing there in ribbons of fabric.

Stella sighed.

"Yeah," she said. "That wasn't the one."

It looked like JONAS wouldn't be going Stelcro quite yet.

THE END

(*really* this time)

*Don't miss a beat! Check out the next
book in the JONAS series.*

KEEPING
IT
REAL

Adapted by Lara Bergen

Based on the series created by Michael Curtis & Roger S. H. Schulman

Based on the episode, "Keeping It Real," Written by Roger S. H. Schulman & Michael Curtis

It was awesome being in JONAS, the hottest
rock band on the planet. As far as Kevin, Joe, and
Nick Lucas could see, they had it all—fame, fans,
fortune, limos, private jets . . . and, of course,
girls. Well, actually, sometimes the girls could get
to be a little much. But what could you expect
when a band was so talented, cute, and, well . . .
awesome?

Since their first album had become a huge hit, the Lucas brothers' lives had changed a lot. Oh, they still lived at home with their mom and dad and little brother, Frankie. And they still went to the same private high school in New Jersey, the Horace Mantis Academy. But just about everything else in their world had gotten much, much, *much* bigger.

They had moved from their old house to a really cool, huge new one. It was a renovated old firehouse, complete with fire poles and an alarm that went off randomly—not great when three teenage boys are trying to catch up on much-needed beauty sleep.

And though the three brothers still shared a room, it was practically the size of a supermarket—complete with a state-of-the-art recording studio and a row of curtained bunks, just like the ones they had installed on their tour bus. Not to mention a food court stocked with all their favorite goodies! Sometimes a little sugar went a long way. . . .

Whenever they wanted to go somewhere, they went—to the Super Bowl or to the World Series or to Tibet to see a solar eclipse. And if they wanted to get there extrafast, they took a helicopter or a private jet. Even better? If they wanted to bring friends, it was no problem. The more, the merrier.

It didn't stop there. The oldest brother, Kevin, loved guitars. He now had not one or two or even a dozen, but *hundreds*, which he kept on a revolving dry-cleaning–style rack in their room.

All these lifestyle changes had taken some time to get used to, and some adjustments were harder than others. It had taken a little while, for example, but most of the girls at school had *finally* gotten used to having three brothers who were exceptionally cute and famous around. The guys still had to run and hide, however, whenever new girls showed up—such as the girls' chorus that had visited just the week before. They were still catching their breath from that one. And so was their bodyguard, the Big Man. Even his size, which was definitely big, couldn't intimidate some fans.

Yep, there was no doubt about it, the Lucas brothers had anything and everything in the world they could ever want (except privacy—but who cared?). They were living out their biggest dreams, and it was great. Though maybe not for everyone . . .